Greedy Gary's Great Surprise!

Photography credit:

Elise Bauer

All other photos: public domain

Written and Illustrated

by

Jeanette Stohlmann

ISBN-978-1790267767

First printing: December 2018

Gary was greedy. If there were three cookies on the plate, Gary grabbed all of them!

Gary was greedy. This often brought his younger

brother to tears!

Gary was greedy. When it was Gary's birthday, he got tons of gifts! But Gary would always ask, "Are there any more?"

Gary was greedy. His parents were worried. One night they sat down for a chat.

"What can we do to help Gary so he is not greedy?" asked his mom, thinking hard.

"Don't worry. I have a plan!" replied his dad. "I am going to take Gary with me on my mission trip to Africa."

The next morning Gary cuddled near his dad on the couch as his dad showed him beautiful pictures of Africa.

"Can I really go with you, Dad?" Gary asked excitedly, "What will we do there?"

"Well," answered his doctor dad, "I'm going to help the sick people and we're going to hand out shoes and teddy bears to the poor children who have no toys. Many of them are sick as well."

"Dad, how many teddy bears are there?" asked Gary.

"Oh, about 200, I think. Why do you ask?"

"Well, Dad, do you think **I** could have **all** those bears to make a teddy bear pyramid for my bedroom?"

"What????!!!" his dad said, shaking his head, "Gary, Gary, Gary. Now it's time for bed because we leave super early in the morning."

Bright and early Gary and his dad boarded a 747-jet airplane to Africa. For the first five minutes Gary enjoyed looking out the window at the fluffy clouds floating in the vast blue sky. But soon he grew tired of it. For the next ten hours he asked his dad every hour, "Are we there yet?" and "What things are you going to buy for me there?"

When they finally arrived, Gary and his dad took a bumpy jeep ride to the village. On the muddy dirt road they passed little huts.

"What are those huts for?" Gary asked.

"That's where people live," answered his dad, "They have no electricity, no heat or air conditioning, and no running water."

Gary saw women crossing the dirt road with jars on their heads. "What's in those jars?" asked Gary.

"Water from the river to drink," answered his dad.

"But isn't the river water dirty?" asked Gary.

"Yes, and that is why many people are sick," his doctor dad replied, "That's why I'm here to help the sick people."

After a short night on a sleeping bag on the hard floor of the village church basement, Gary's dad woke early to work at the village hospital. Gary was too tired to get up because of jet lag after the twelve-hour trip.

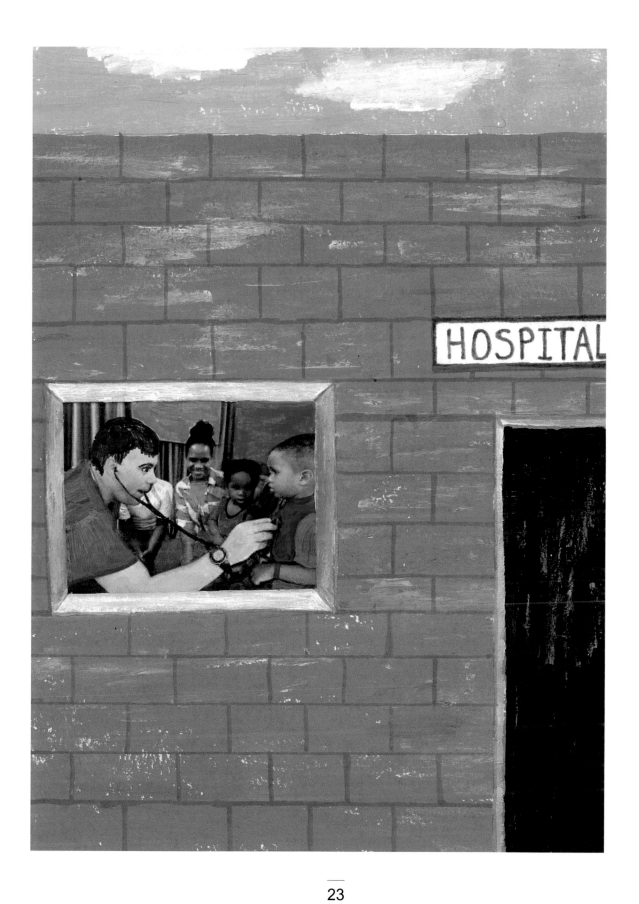

At noon, sunlight streamed through the open church basement window and a red rooster roused Gary from his sleep. The church basement floor was covered with sleeping bags from all the other mission trip volunteers who had already put in a morning's work.

Some of the volunteers helped at the hospital. Some of the volunteers repaired the church. Some of the volunteers dug wells for clean water.

When Gary's dad arrived back at the church, Gary whined about wanting to eat at his favorite restaurant.

"They don't have McDonald's here," explained his dad, "so just try the chicken curry, son."

"But I don't like it," complained Gary.

"Well, then you will get very hungry, son," said his Dad matter-of-factly.

After about an hour, Gary ate the chicken curry and decided it was rather good after all.

Gary watched his dad and the volunteers load boxes of

shoes and teddy bears into the battered green pickup truck.

When Gary and his dad arrived at the drop-off place, lots of

village children were already eagerly lining the road!

As Gary's dad passed out shoes, he said, "Jesus loves you" to each child, so Gary copied him.

"Jesus loves you," said Gary to each one. Gary was surprised as to how much fun it was to see their faces light up with smiles! He was also surprised that the children did not have any shoes on their feet!

It was fun handing out the shoes! But quickly, the box

of shoes became empty and there were still children

looking up eagerly for their pairs of shoes!

Gary sat down by a palm tree and cried, "Dad, I had

enough shoes at home for the rest of those children. If only

I had brought them with me."

"Next time, son," said Gary's dad opening the big box

of bears.

Gary and his dad handed out 200 teddy bears! The delighted children had never seen a stuffed toy before! They skipped away joyfully, hugging their bears!

As Gary and his dad were about to drive the green pickup back to the church, Gary's dad glanced in the side-view mirror. A small boy looked up at them, softly pleading, "Please may I have a bear? I saw all the other children with bears. I could not run as fast, because I have a bad leg. I hope I am not too late."

Gary looked at the small boy's sad face and then at his poor crooked leg. "I'll give him my bear," whispered Gary to his dad.

"Are you sure you want to do this, son?" Gary's dad asked, surprised.

"Yes!" exclaimed Gary, and before his dad could say anything more, Gary ran like the wind, down the long dirt road to the church to get his favorite teddy bear.

In a flash, Gary returned all out of breath and handed the small boy his special teddy bear. Right away, the small boy's face lit up like a Christmas tree!

"Jesus loves you," assured Gary giving the small boy a hug.

"I can feel His love," said the small boy. "Thank you so much! I think God sent you here to tell me He loves me. Thank you!"

Gary was all smiles when he climbed into the back of the old green pickup. "Dad," began Gary, "I feel better **giving** away my bear than **getting** all those gifts on my birthday. Why is that, Dad?"

"Well, son, that's because the Bible says it is more blessed or happy to give than to receive," explained his dad, "You're happy because you made someone else happy by sharing God's love!"

"Dad," Gary said excitedly, "when I get home, I am going to send my extra shoes and toys to the mission here!"

"Wonderful, Gary!" beamed his dad, "Today God gave you the **gift of giving**!"

Note to Parents and Grown-ups:

The Bible verse, John 3:16, says it all: *"For God so loved the world that he **gave**..."*

God calls each one of us to imitate this kind of amazing love!

It's not just certain people God loves, but the whole world! This is a tall order and we can only fulfill it with the help of the Holy Spirit!

God can change selfishness into selflessness! He pours His amazing love into our hearts through His Word and Sacraments.

Because of God's infinite supply of love, we can rest assured that we will always have enough love to go around!

God loved us and gave His Son, Jesus, to pay for our sins, die, and come alive again on the third day. Jesus promised to be with us always and we can talk to Him in prayer anytime of the day or night. Jesus said, *"Greater love has no one than this: to lay down one's life for one's friends." John 15:13*

Prayer:
   Dear Jesus, thank you for dying for me to save me. Fill me with Your unselfish love that I may share Your great love with others! Amen.

I John 4:7 "Dear friends, let us love one another, for love comes from God. Everyone who loves has been born of God and knows God."

James 1:17 "Every good and perfect gift is from above, coming down from the Father of the heavenly lights, who does not change like shifting shadows."

+

Made in the USA
Monee, IL
25 September 2020

42396126R00029